TIM BURTON'S
THE NIGHTMARE BEFORE CHRISTMAS

SCRIPT ADAPTATION
Alessandro Ferrari

LAYOUTS, PENCILS & INKS
Massimiliano Narciso

COLOR
Kawaii Studio

LETTERS
Edizioni BD

ABDOBOOKS.COM

Reinforced library bound edition published in 2022 by Spotlight, a division of ABDO, PO Box 398166, Minneapolis, Minnesota 55439. Spotlight produces high-quality reinforced library bound editions for schools and libraries. Published by agreement with Disney Enterprises, Inc.

Printed in the United States of America, North Mankato, Minnesota.
042021
092021

THIS BOOK CONTAINS
RECYCLED MATERIALS

Library of Congress Control Number: 2020947969

Publisher's Cataloging-in-Publication Data

Names: Ferrari, Alessandro, author. | Narciso, Massimiliano, illustrator.
Title: Tim burton's the nightmare before christmas / by Alessandro Ferrari ; illustrated by Massimiliano Narciso.
Description: Minneapolis, Minnesota : Spotlight, 2022. | Series: Disney classics
Summary: Pumpkin King Jack Skellington's merry mission to spread the joy of Christmas puts Santa in jeopardy and creates a nightmare for good little boys and girls everywhere.
Identifiers: ISBN 9781532148033 (lib. bdg.)
Subjects: LCSH: Night before Christmas (Motion picture)--Juvenile fiction. | Skeleton--Juvenile fiction. | Halloween--Juvenile fiction. | Christmas--Juvenile fiction. | Kidnapping--Juvenile fiction. | Graphic novels--Juvenile fiction.
Classification: DDC 741.5--dc23

Spotlight

A Division of ABDO
abdobooks.com

Welcome, dear readers, to [...] where everybody screams, scares and loves a good trick!

This is our town the town of vampires, witches and hanging trees, clowns without a face and nightmares smiling from the moon...

And the most special resident

What is this place?

I've never seen so many different colors! And people! They throw snowballs and have fun, they kiss...

But why? They smile, they laugh, they look happy! There are no monsters under their beds, no witches, no vampires.

laughing and singing! Am I dreaming?
...under mistletoe and cover trees with electric lights?!

I've never felt this warmth in my heart.
I want to understand. I want to know what this place
is and who... he... is...

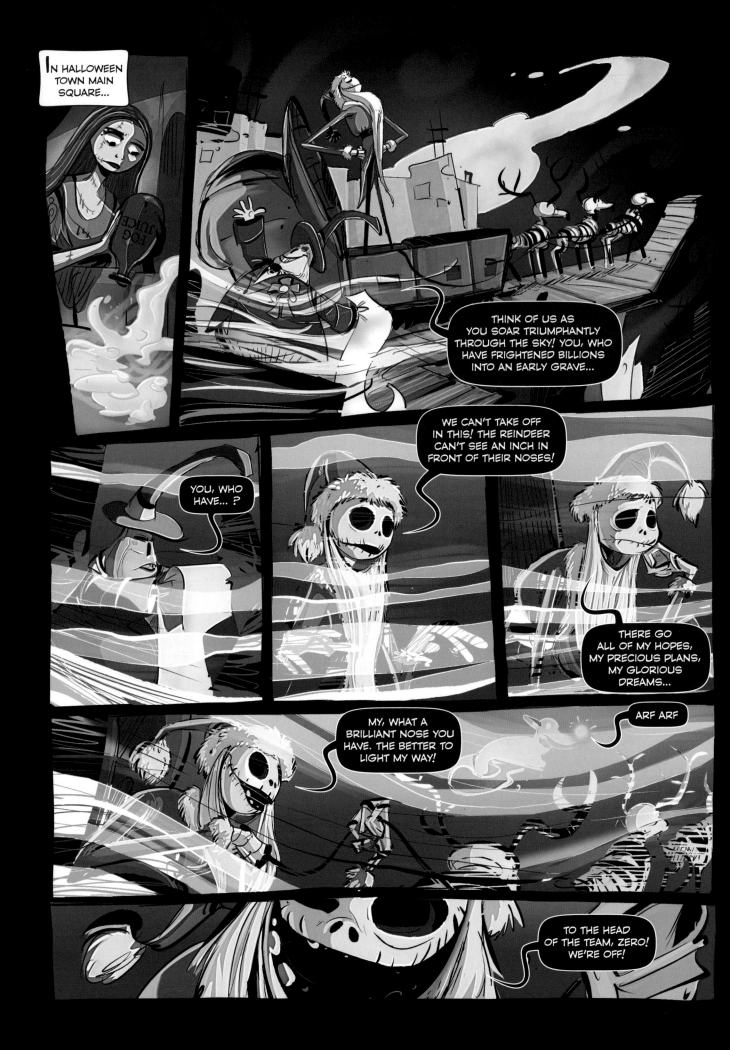

"You don't look like yourself, Jack—not at all."
"It couldn't be more wonderful!"

—SALLY AND JACK

DISNEY CLASSICS

COLLECT THEM ALL